The Irritating Gentleman

Gentleman

and Other Creative Writing Prompts and Responses

The Irritating Gentleman

and Other Creative Writing Prompts and Responses

Edited by Marina Lambrou

KU
PRESS

Typeset in Hobeaux and Questa Grande

Editorial and Design by Kingston University Press Publishing Assistant: Yasmien Ibrahim

KINGSTON UNIVERSITY PRESS
Kingston University
Penrhyn Road
Kingston-upon-Thames
KT1 2EE

Contents

Acknowledgements

Editing a book is a collaborative affair with many people involved in the final output. I would like to thank Emma Tait, Course Leader for MA Publishing and Publisher for Kingston University Press, who thought editing a collection of student work was a great idea and was invaluable in the early discussions. I would also like to thank Yasmien Ibrahim, a student of MA Publishing at Kingston University, for supporting me during this process and for the book's front cover. I gave Yasmien the brief and she interpreted this beautifully into an original piece of artwork that welcomes readers into multi-layered story worlds.

Of course, without the creative works, this book would not exist, so I would like to thank the BA Creative Writing students from the 2023–24 class of CW5003 *Content, Form and Creativity* at Kingston University for their original works of fiction that formed this unique collection.

Contributors

Zara Auckbaraullee
Sadie Brett
Sofia Camara-Martins
Adelina Cazacutu
Noah Chandler
Ayah Cueto
Alice Da Costa
Shai Duggal
Giften Etienne
Lily Ferret
Lilly Grant
Joe Hester
Danica Ignacio
Amanda Mangolini
Eulyn Raguindin
Tye Rajapura
Sinnead Singson
Harper Stringer
Zenon Teasdale
Theo Vaughan
Sofija Vipule
Bella Weerasinghe

Introduction

'To write is to be a linguist,' asserts the creative writer and stylistician Jeremy Scott (2014: 423) who goes on to explain that to engage in creative practice, the writer must engage with the mechanics of language best done through the study of stylistics, or literary linguistics. It is necessary to know how linguistic choices and clause-patterns, for example, create style and genre, as well as the meanings and effects they communicate (whether these reside in the text or in the reader's interpretation). Through the discipline of stylistics, writers – and readers – can gain important insights into how texts are created that they can then apply to their own writing. This collection of new and original fictional works is a clear example of this. *'The Irritating Gentleman' and Other Creative Writing Prompts and Responses* is the culmination of creative work produced by students, specifically the class of 2023–24, studying stylistics in a creative writing degree course. For most of these students, stylistics was a new subject and their introduction to the subject began with useful definitions such as the one offered by Giovanelli and Mason (2018: 2):

> **Stylistics:** the study of style; a discipline within the field of linguistics that examines how every linguistic choice can influence the overall effect of a text.

Knowledge of stylistics and of the metalanguage – the terms used to describe language – are also key for students to be able to discuss, describe and explain their writing, whether in the classroom context or, and this is the goal, with their future agent and publisher, in a confident and persuasive manner.

'The Irritating Gentleman' and Other Creative Writing Prompts and Responses is organised into five sections, under the various creative writing prompts given to students during the semester, with their responses. Creative Writing Prompt 1, This is a Photograph of Me, was inspired by Margaret Atwood's 1964 poem of the same title, a poem which appears at first to describe a calm, picturesque surrounding, focalised through a first person narration. That is until readers are told 'The photograph was taken the day after I drowned', halfway through the poem. This startling revelation destabilises the reading of the earlier part of the poem to make the reader question their interpretation of what is real and literal, and what is metaphorical. Who then, is 'me'? Who is narrating this improbable event and experience? Who has taken the photo, and more broadly, what does the poem mean? The discussion in class, which asked students to focus on stylistic choices, emotive language, words within the same semantic fields, cohesive chains, etc. to make sense of the poem, encouraged students to interpret this poem (and any they go on to read), in a way that made sense to them because there is no one answer. (See also Toolan, 1988 for his discussion points on analysing this poem.) For the creative writing task, students were asked to write the first two stanzas of a poem or the opening paragraph of a novel entitled 'This is a Photograph of Me' that could be read as literal or figurative and based on a real or fictional person or setting.

Creative Writing Prompt 2, My Autobiography, required students to write the first paragraph of their autobiography using excerpts of text analysed in class as inspiration for their writing. That week's focus on language explored both sentence structure and lexical choices, including foregrounding, to understand how stylistic choices create style and genre. The texts given out in class for the creative writing prompts were the opening sentences from two autobiographies – one real and one fictional – by the actor Terence Stamp (1987) *Stamp Album*, written in a rather jaunty style, and William Boyd's (1987) *The New Confessions*, which begins with the more sombre 'My first act on entering this world was to kill my mother.' As well as analysing the features of the texts, students were asked to identify: i. which one they enjoyed most and would choose to read; and ii. which autobiography is real and which is fictional. (Not all students identified the fictional text but most preferred it to the factually based autobiography).

A lesson that looked at narration and point of view was the context for the writing prompt in Creative Writing Prompt 3, 'The Irritating Gentleman' by Berthold Woltze. Students were presented with various linguistic techniques for narrating a story to understand different diegetic levels and how events are focalised for a subjective and (un)reliable experience. Students were also introduced to the notion of *mind style* (Fowler, 1986; Semino, 2002) and ideological point of view to understand how to give their characters a unique voice. For the creative writing task, Berthold Woltze's 1874 painting 'The Irritating Gentleman' was presented as an ekphrastic prompt that uses visual art as a literary device to inspire students to create their fictional work. Students were asked to write a creative piece based on Woltze's painting. The piece could be narrated by any one of the three characters in the painting and represented through speech, thought or both. Alternatively, students could provide an outline of a plot, with details of the characters and their speech or thoughts. In either option, students were asked to consider the following when creating their story world: genre, style, the principle of minimal departure, narration and point of view, and mind style for presenting speech and thought.

The fourth activity under Creative Writing Prompt 4, *Writing Dialogue: An Argument*, followed on from a class that explored dialogue as discourse, using the sociolinguistic model of Conversation Analysis (Sacks et al., 1974) for the structure of turn-taking, to analyse character relationships through their interactions. Students analysed texts containing dialogue for features of powerplay and politeness that contributed to creating authentic representations of speech, which they could then apply to their own creative writing. One of the texts analysed in class was an excerpt from *Richard III* (Act IV. Scene ii) that exemplified the powerful versus powerless interaction between the newly crowned King Richard and Lord Buckingham (see Short, 1996). The creative writing prompt required students to write their own dialogue in the form of an argument. Using *Richard III* as a reference point, they could either rewrite the dialogue set in the present as an argument between the Princes William and Harry or write a piece based on a real argument they had experienced. Students were asked to consider how they would present the turn-taking, i.e. as direct speech, free direct speech, as a screenplay, etc.

The final Creative Writing Prompt 5, *Your Fairy Tale*, was a creative writing activity that followed a workshop on the short story to examine the characteristics of this form of writing, with fairy tales – the literary appropriations of oral folk tales – offering the most prototypical form of fictional storytelling. Students also learnt about the historical development of well-known traditional fairy tales attributed to Perault and the Brothers Grimm to understand how changes in plot reflected the ideology, moral codes and general cultural expectations of their time (see Bettleheim, 1976; Zipes, 1991). For the creative writing activity, students were asked to rewrite a well-known fairy tale making their version as original and as unconventional as they could but readers should still be able to recognise the plot and characters. Students were asked to think about some of the creative writing prompts given out in class, e.g. by starting their story in the middle, with a flashback, choosing a different narrator / point of view, updating the setting, undermining schematic expectations, etc.

I hope you enjoy the prompts and responses produced by the students and that this collection will inspire you with your own creative writing.

References

Atwood, M. (1964) 'This is a Photograph of Me'. In *The Circle Game*. Canada: House of Anansi Press Ltd.

Bettelheim, B (1976) *The uses of Enchantment, the Meaning and Importance of fairy Tales*. London: Puffin.

Boyd, W. (1987) *The New Confessions*. London: Penguin. Fowler, R (1986) *Linguistic Criticism*. Oxford: Oxford University Press.

Giovanelli, M. and Mason, J. (2018) *The Language of Literature* Oxford: Oxford University Press.

Sacks, H., Schegloff, A. and Jefferson, G. (1974) 'A simplest systematics for the organization of turn-taking for conversation'. *Language*. 50 (4): 696–735.

Scott, J (2014) 'Creative writing and stylistics'. In M. Burke (ed.) *The Routledge Handbook of Stylistics*. Pp. 423–439. London: Routledge.

Semino, E (2002) 'Cognitive stylistics and mind style'. In E. Semino and J. Culpeper (eds) *Cognitive Stylistics, Language and Cognition in Text Analysis*. Pp. 95–122. Amsterdam: John Benjamins.

Short, M. (1996) *Exploring the language of Poems, Plays and Prose*. Harlow, England: Longman.

Stamp, T. (1987) *Stamp Album*. London: Bloomsbury.

Toolan, M. (1998) *Language in Literature. An Introduction to Stylistics*. London: Arnold.

Zipes, J. (1991) *Fairy Tales and the Art of Subversion*. London: Routledge.

CREATIVE WRITING PROMPT 1

This is a Photograph of Me

Write the first two stanzas of a poem or the opening paragraph of a novel entitled 'This is a photograph of me'. It can be literal or figurative and based on a real or fictional person or setting. . . It's up to you.

This is a Photograph of Me

I suppose I look happy.
Wearing ivory and tulle
Standing tall – defiant.
I'm giving my vows, my oaths,
(*Nothing but the truth*)
Adorned and embellished,
Soft lies and soft lace.
I am captured,
Enraptured–

The flash illuminates my
Blood red cheeks,
Deep purple shadows line my eyes.
My hands are clasped arounda broken string of pearls–
(*My evidence*)
And their vicious marks on my neck remain.

Bella Weerasinghe

This is a Photograph of Me

Forget how many. The sigh of a word developing.
Printing photo from crumbled rose petal.
Clenched so tight through sighing, it forms a basin
and wrapped within it is only an idea.
If even an idea, but it yellows as it sets.

The photo I hold can't speak to others.
If only speak – it relieves itself
If only speak – reveals a realer glance, or so it smells.
So, it somehow cremates before the ashes
form their tower, that takes a delicate slip before it breaks.

Harper Stringer

This is a Photograph of Me

Of what should have been.
Pupils purer than them all
Accompanied by a gentle smile of touching warmth
that slowly fades as the years go by.
Time ticking. That's one certainty.

The clock stops in my dreams
But not in reality.
Friends coming and going
Family departing
If I could turn back time
To life in through those pure pupils.

Joe Hester

This is a Photograph of Me

Red eyes and bright eyes,
cheeks up to the corners,
arm and shoulders.

Date stamped in yellow,
pictures from before,
all of us four.

Bone sand whips while blue waves ebb,
my eyes were fuller then,
of what was and could've been.

Noah Chandler

This is a Photograph of Me

A moment captured in time and space
Preserving the beauty of foreverness.
A pair would wed,
their vows they'd speak.

One,
A spirit so free and pure.
The other,
A heart now cruel and cool.
If you listen closely to the secrets whispered,
A love that's lost is revealed,
A love that's me.

Alice Da Costa

This is a Photograph of Me

A chill breeze with warm glows,
A morning kiss and a bird's hello
Gentle graze where the flowers glow,
Rough strokes where the tall grass grows.

Sweet little hums in those lonesome strolls,
A listless smile with eyes of soul
Kind streams with subtle strains,
Titbit whispers in their strides
And the mellow hums occluding with every glide.

Ayah Cueto

This is a Photograph of Me

Or maybe of the potential
That I ought to
But cannot see
Of all the things
I'd like and strive to be;
But when I look,
All that I see
Is a hollow shell
A mellow soul,
A prickly touch,
A wandering mind and a dreamy gaze,
A string of words that fall from my lips
Like a spell, a curse;
All I see –
Is a photograph
of me.

Sofija Vipule

This is a Photograph of Me

This is a photograph of me
And everything I was
And I will never be.

In one small frame
An unmade bed, orange and green
A decorated chest, a treasure hunt
Promises of adventures, dreams, swords and dragons
It's all gone.

Smiling at the camera, shy, out of place
Is she still there?

Amanda Mangolini

This is a Photograph of Me

I am dancing
to Claire De Lune.
My name is Claire. Or is it?
The éclairs are following me.
He bought them. They are not mine.
He said: 'A little something for your birthday.'
Claire, I love you.

Flip the photo (upside down).
And you will notice my toes
dipped in moonlight.
My name is Lune. Or is it?
The light is following me.
He cast it. It is not mine.
He said: 'You look beautiful tonight.'
But, Lune, I no longer love you.

Turn the photo (over).
My name is Claire De Lune. Or is it?

Adelina Cazacutu

Liquor

At least that's what I remember it to be.
His face is stubbled and ever so slightly blemished.
His hair is long and glossy; it almost looks varnished.
I vaguely remember the party whence this was taken,
After he hit the liquor, his stance and speech was shaken.
He is smiling.
He. . . Well, he is probably smiling.
He probably can't drink like that anymore
Unless he wants his cortex pickled.
Probably. He might actually be able to
But I haven't tried it.

Theo Vaughan

This is a Photograph of Me

when you pick up the papery film of my body,
do you feel the weight of every word you whispered to it?
or am I as light as you convinced me I am?
go on then – rip up the dyed polymer that's been made of my skin,
feel the stress of having me between your fingers once more, show
the audience how well you glue me back together when you're done.
hang me from the yarn that's clinging onto the crown moulding of
your childhood bedroom, take me down when you move out then
put me back up on new walls
so you can tell the story of that girl you knew once: how kind you
speak of her despite the fact that you've grown apart – you gentle,
gentle god.

Danica Ignacio

This is a Photograph of Me

You scream these six words–
affirmation for your own eardrums,
Smuggled in disguise as a statement to me
My brows crow at the disturbed shapes.

Wet lipped, slicked,
curved and pinched, nip and tuck
As the person who felt your peach fuzz on theirs,
This is a photograph of you?

Sadie Brett

This is a Photograph of Me

Lily has fireflies dancing around in her room.
They're only lights that she sees with her eyes
brighter than her first smile.
She loved the drawings she drew against her walls.
She thought that these drawings would come
to life one day.
She has magic hands.

And I thought fireflies only came out at night.
My eyes are like cameras, not wanting to miss her.
And not wanting to ruin her.
Because if I did, she would disappear.
My mind would become a trapped door.
For I wish for her to stay alive.

Eulyn Raguindin

This is a Photograph of Me

It hangs above my bed, plasters the walls,
wedges itself 'tween me and mirror.
I see it when I close my eyes.

Lead paint and gilded glory,
downturned eyes and folded hands,
draped like a girl with the poise of a lady.

Sinnead Singson

This is a Photograph of Me

This is a photograph of me that everyone has seen, but nobody sees me.

There in the foreground is the foliage
And the background, buildings.
I'm over there. Look, where I'm pointing.

If you look really hard, you can see that little speck between the
clouds; it's a Boeing 747, which can 'carry 467 passengers at peak
capacity'.

If you weren't there you'd never know
How the b— blew.
But oh yes, I was right there.

The sweet nectar of the blooming flowers was heavy next to the
park and the buzzing sound was near deafening.

Sombre sorts will say to you dramatically
How the buds bloomed
In a story that mentions me briefly.

Nevertheless, there I am, soon to give a statement on how tragic it
was and that nobody could have foreseen it.

Everyone reading the paper has seen my story,

But nobody sees me.
I am just as important as them.

(This piece is a work of satire.)

Lilly Grant

This is a Photograph of Me

Hopeless romantics write no sonnets, yet I
have nurtured this feeling into a lovable nuisance.
Found in silence, hushed to sleep with
compulsive lullabies when
loved ones set to Heaven – it *must be a distant land for*
none returned. Perhaps no one ever loved you to return. But *I* love you. *I*
loved you through health and sickness, love and hate your reluctance
to accept that we were made for each other. *Soulmates.*
Crimson chains bind you to the scent of iron, sweet with intimate discipline.
I love the real you – Human. Yet you think yourself
unworthy of the title "Human". Why? Are others' opinions more
important than mine?
They don't love you.

I love you. . . Human.
Die for me in a lovers' suicide.

Sofia Camara-Martins

CREATIVE WRITING PROMPT 2

My Autobiography

Thinking about the real and fictional autobiographical excerpts we analysed in today's class, write the first paragraph of your autobiography.

Oven Baby

Unless you want to go from your birth, finding a place to start talking about your life is immeasurably difficult. My memory also has all the date retention of a goldfish with a rusty sieve, so I can't just pick a day, age, or even a year to begin with.

Let's start from when I was in early primary, playing pretend with all the other girls, and being told I was a baby trapped in an oven.

Lilly Grant

My Autobiography

My due date was supposed to be the 24th of June 2004. The doctors told my mother that I was the wrong way up in the womb and that in the event of a natural birth, I would come out feet first. So, they scheduled a caesarean two days later and on the 26th of June 2004, I was born in the unfortunate location of Portsmouth, England with the name Theo Atticus Apperley Vaughan. An English boy with a Greek first and middle name, a Welsh last name that nobody knew how to spell for the first twelve years of my life and, according to Scottish tradition, my mother's unconventional West-English maiden name was sandwiched between all of them: great start.

Theo Vaughan

My Autobiography

On a random Thursday, mid-morning, the doctors cut open my mother, and there I was, my mother's baby. I had an easy childhood, blind to anything further than my own nose, enabled by my own naivety and stupidity. I can't recall much of my childhood in detail – it's all a blur of colours and sounds, all intertwined with one another, one memory bleeding into another: sunny afternoons spent playing pretend under the scorching sun; my all-white school uniform; my older brother, with mischievous plans that got us into trouble more often than not; my mother, now smaller than me, seemed to me larger than life back then; and my father, all jokes and teasing.

Tye Rajapura

My Autobiography

Sunhaila and Sumeer Duggal had very simple reasons for choosing to adopt me in November 2004. They couldn't resist my big eyes, small nose and round face. They took one long look at me and decided they were going to take me into their home and raise me. They wanted a daughter for the longest time, and after a decade of pain, heartache and decision making, they welcomed me into their family.

Shai Duggal

Confessions of an Island Girl

Auckbaraullee. That's my surname. It's difficult to pronounce – if you overthink it. *Ok-burrow-lee*. That's how you pronounce it. Since as young as I can remember, I have been told that it's an unusual name, and perhaps this is why I have grown to despise it – something I pity myself for, because such a name holds such history of those who came before me within my bloodline. So unusual? Yes. Common? Definitely not. But known? Very. 'Auckbaraullee' is a very well-known name, one that is recognised greatly in Mauritius. That's where I'm from, a tropical island in the Indian Ocean. The land of the dodos.

Zara Auckbaraullee

My Autobiography

At my moment of birth, my dad decided that I was not delicate enough to be a 'Lily'. Yet that is my name and, growing up, I have found that lilies are so much more than what they are perceived to be. Some will poison, some will heal, some represent death and others rebirth. I am all of these things wrapped together, yet I cannot represent its purity.

Lily Ferret

Born to Drink. Forced to Piss it Out.

The sweet, coconut creamy sounds of the pina colada song seemed to soothe my mother after birth. It's one of her favourites and now it's mine.

My half brain was born to enjoy the simple things in life like yoga, fruity cocktails and silly media shows. Melodies that comfort, the ones that touch the soul. A real human being. I drive into the depths of whimsy nature and escape a silly man. In a way, birth is similar. An escape, a new dawn, a new life. So, come with me and escape.

Zenon Teasdale

Sofija: A Tale from Ephesus

Before my parents found out whether they were expecting a girl or a boy, my father was certain of one thing: I was to be named Sofija. He had decided this on their honeymoon to Turkey, where he'd set foot into the ancient ruins of Ephesus, lined with statues of the many gods and goddesses of an ancient reality. He had gazed upon them with great care, until he saw the statue of the goddess Sophia – the goddess of wisdom. And so, having unknowingly set her up with high expectations before she was even born, the young Sofija would spend her life striving to live up to her name. And now, in everything I do, I strive to make the young Sofija proud.

Sofija Vipule

My Autobiography

As a Filipino, I was gifted with a name that would rarely be used. Filipino culture cherishes the use of nicknames as expressions of endearment or simply out of preference. Throughout my 20 years of life, I have been bestowed with many nicknames, some in Tagalog and some in English – each holding equal importance to me. I've been called Até (older sister), Whore, Anak (my child), Useless, Bunso (my baby), Ganda (beauty) and, most importantly, Bunak. This last one, Bunak, holds a special place in my heart. It was given to me by none other than my grandmother. The name she chose was not only a playful abbreviation but also translates to 'milk child'. The idiosyncrasies of my culture have always served as a constant reminder to not only embrace myself fully but also to grow into something more, allowing me to detach from the toxicity that sometimes accompanies this unique culture.

Ayah Cueto

Opening extract from 'The Brass Wakes The Trumpet' by Harper Stringer, published 2035

Phantoms were whistling, stopping as they came through. But first:

A numb hand must make its voyage across the sheets when it unexpectedly falls where a table ought to be. Through closed eyes, the thing between the walls is a map of blurred outlines that light occasionally scolds through. But hold on... that chair is no longer sat on, that wall no longer painted with an illustration on the wall. That plane from a Maurice Sendak book, it's now spun itself away. The bed of crinkled lilies transformed to bedsheets, smells only of indifferent exhaustion. It's not that room anymore. This can be made clear when those eyes open – my eyes. 'Yesterday I left home,' I remember, and these new exteriors aren't a silent wallpaper – they scream as if asking me to flip them a coin. How useless yesterday seems; how seamlessly I have become another!

Then with the understanding of where I am achieved, what better time to get up? Any other time, to tell the truth. Instead, I lay for a while contemplating making a cup of tea, but my new flatmates are in the kitchen and I'm as made up as a battlefield. Those two steps out of bed and I face the mirror image. It's strange to see that I had the same body that I always did, but when it goes into the world it's an empty vessel where a mirror stands, reflecting only what stands before it.

Harper Stringer

My Autobiography

Every evening is cold in January, but I provided warmth to my mother on the last day of the month at approximately 5:30pm. I'm told that getting to the hospital in labour was a bit tricky, as my father had a broken leg at the time from a nasty football challenge a couple of weeks prior and was unable to drive. Mum laughs now, but it wasn't a pleasant situation at the time. Brought home to my older brother, I would eventually end up as the middle child two years later. In a sandwich of siblings, some might think of it as a burden, but it's beyond a blessing. Especially as an adult. One main lingering thought on my birthday that's post-Christmas and New Year's is that it can be a bit depressing, can't it?

Joe Hester

My Autobiography

My parents disagree about when I was born. My ma swears I was born around noon, when the sun was high in the sky and beat on the window of her hospital room. My dad insists I was born at 14:22 exactly, a near reversal of my birthday. My dad's rather fond of near reversals, I think, since my own name is a near reversal of his. Dennis and Sinnead, two peas in a pod up until puberty.

Sinnead Singson

A Snippet of My Autobiography

I remember Christmas Day, when I was five or six years old, at my grandparent's house.

Even before the renovation of the kitchen, the house was too small to contain all our family reunited. And Italian families are big if you count all the cousins, aunts and uncles.

My grandmother used to set up a big table that went from one side of the kitchen into the living room, across the corridor, to the front of the front door.

There were laughs, passionate politic debates, some arguing and lots and lots of food.

Sadly, most of those people are not here anymore.

Amanda Mangolini

My Autobiography

I have played the piano for a very long time. But the one thing I would like to do, besides *just* playing the piano, is to perform in a concert hall. I've never done it before, but I have seen it done before. 'Beloved Clara' from Lucy Parham has been one of those concerts that has moved me. I'm not the kind of person to usually explore classical music outside of listening to it from a Spotify playlist. But hearing the music being played by Lucy Parham on the piano felt like space.

Eulyn Raguindin

You Can't Chandle Me

Congratulations, you bought a copy of my autobiography, *You Can›t Chandle Me: An Autobiography of Noah Michael Chandler.* It all started one fateful day in April. Then, nine months later, I was born. The doctor took me in his gloved hands, had one look at me and said, 'Yeesh.' No, not actually. But in the hospital, my brother, Nick, pointed at my mom holding me in her arms and exclaimed, 'Put that baby down!' My parents named me Noah, which apparently means 'peace'. I think that's what they were hoping for.

Noah Chandler

Subject 120903

Subject no. 120903 refused to write an autobiography in a language it cannot speak. *English*, it said, *é muita areia para o meu caminhão*. It is therefore the courtesy of Management X – overseer of subject 120903 – to document its first encounter with life via what's left of the records from twenty years ago.

Subject 120903 demonstrated its first partum abnormality when, unlike the rest of its species, it consumed the amniotic fluid kept in its glass-like incubator. This phenomenon cannot be explained through science; it is also probable that it will remain so for no other subject has displayed the same or similar anomaly while taking their first breath. However, it was not unusual for it to have been born before its due date – four days to be exact. The aforementioned has no logical reason, however, it is likely that subject 120903 may have been tired of being fed lactobacillus bulgaricus (otherwise known as 'yoghurt') and coffee – the latter of which subject 120903 does not resonate with post-partum.

Sofia Camara-Martins

My Autobiography

I started out in the same concrete building as the rest of the litter – between my mother, my father and the old lady that delivered me (who I still see every other Christmas). I snuck my way into a lucky number 3, slithered right through the crack between yesterday and tomorrow.

I took three letters from each parent and then another four from my aunt for safe keeping.

With a head full of hair and limbs too frail to fight anything, I held my breath for the first time.

Danica Ignacio

The Iris Files

Every single summer of my perfect childhood was spent surrounded by strawberry fields – both the pick-your-own and the Cath Kidston varieties. The entirety of Surrey was, to me, just one great big farm shop after another and I was just a cheese-straw obsessed child going absolutely ham for the *Garson's Farm* baked goods section. New Year's Day meant long, wet, windy walks on a beach and Boxing Day meant driving up to Bedford for the Weerasinghe Birthday Christmas Anniversary Extravaganza. Life was great, life was simple, and nothing ever changed.

Bella Weerasinghe

CREATIVE WRITING PROMPT 3

'The Irritating Gentleman'
Berthold Woltze (1874)

Write a creative piece based on Woltze's painting in 150–200 words.

Your piece can be narrated by *any one of the three characters* in the painting and represented through speech, thought or both;
or
Provide an outline of the plot. Who are the characters in the story? What is happening? What is the character saying. . . thinking?

Consider the following when creating your story world: *genre, style, the principle of minimal departure, narration and point of view; mind style* for speech styles; how to present speech and thought, etc.

The Irritating Gentleman

He and I are similar in this way: curious. The smoke from his pipe settles on my cheek. I feel a foreign sense of disgust and dehumanising loss of control. He speaks to me and I hear nothing, but if you asked me, I'd say the sounds are close to a blabber of 'give us a smile' and 'where ya off to'.

I think about what I would say if I were to respond to him, how to politely say I'm off to see my mother in a casket. Although I doubt it matters where I'm going really, as long as I reveal to him a secret – let it be of whatever sort, to break the mystery of the sweet girl on the train.

Like I said though, he and I are similar. I think, if you placed an injured bird on my lap at this very moment, I would also compare his frail body to my healthy one. I would lean towards him, examine under his wings and run a finger down his beak. Cover him in the scent of my tobacco so he can be as similar to me as possible and make of him a disciple.

I would wonder what destination must be so important for this bird to injure himself, paint himself vulnerable.

My daydream breaks when I feel a finger touch behind my ear. I flinch and he laughs. This is where he and I differ, where we draw the line between indulgence and interests. He beckons his friend to join him and he touches me again – my arm this time. I flinch again and shuffle closer to the window. I am hot wax and he is testing how much of me he can take before his skin touches flame.

I am restricted, classified – he yearns for a truth that he thinks can be found under my skirt. He wants to be applauded, credited for successful discovery and I am his fossil, his fuel and feed.

Danica Ignacio

The Irritating Gentleman

My God, I wish he would leave her alone. I wish he would stop speaking altogether, but I suppose that's why Stockwell hired him, because he lacks the shame that would prevent any ordinary man from approaching even the most obviously uninterested parties. In the professional setting, I'm not so bothered by that, I actually marvel at his unstoppable conversational inertia; he is like the locomotive scraping down the track, chugging toward clients with mechanised confidence, his superficial assertions billowing above him. But, like most men in this business, he is all too happy to brandish his professional skill (that being his ability to be an abrasive agent, withering people down until they comply) outside of the professional area. Here that is now. This young lady is dressed in black and not for, I assume, a costume party. And yet, on he goes, Stockwell's prize horse, blabbering on to this poor girl.

Noah Chandler

48

The Irritating Gentleman

What an irritating gentleman, you thought, as you watched his pitiful attempts at conversation land like drunken punches into thin air. The strange fellow was hanging off the back of his seat like a schoolboy, directing stale ale breath towards Lady Emilia. Although you were gladly out of the line of fire from his cigar stink and his constant pomp and spittle, the lady was suffering. She had been bundled onto the train right after the funeral and was well on her way to Witherton Hall. The Viscount had given you strict instruction – you must not make yourself known to the lady, but shadow her from a safe distance, to make sure of not only her safety from others, but from herself.

Lady Emilia was clearly in mourning – the whole carriage was trying not to eavesdrop on her quiet tears. All but this man, at least. As you watched him lean dangerously close to her, twirling his moustache between dusty fingers, you suppressed the urge to rip it right off. Unless she was in immediate, fatal danger, you had been urged to sit tight and quietly observe. The lady turned away from the man, wiping her eyes discreetly on a handkerchief, reaching for something. . .

A flash of silver. The man crumpled, snoring.

You smiled to yourself as you realised just why you had been instructed to keep your distance.

Bella Weerasinghe

The Irritating Gentleman

Oh!

    . . . My apologies, sir. You startled me.

    Hm? Oh, yes, it's my aunt, she—

    . . . Yes, that is correct.

    How observant.

    Sir, I find the irritation of your cigar to be quite. . .

    No, please do not put it out on my behalf! I—

    I am afraid not.

    Not in the slightest.

    I would prefer you don't go to such lengths. You needn't prove anything. No—

    Good lord, man! Can't you leave the poor girl alone? She is grieving!

    No, I must be the one to apologise. If I may ask, who is it you have lost?

    Up in the northern territories?

    And you loved her dearly.

    Why, would I be a good vicar if I were not observant enough to tell a distraught woman from one in perfect sensibilities? Why—

    I say! She told you to put the blasted thing out and you shall listen!

    No, my dear, he must learn to be sensitive to his surroundings. Are you in knowledge of Corinthians 13?

    Not in the slightest?

Well, sweet child, let me procure my Holy Book, you shall find it soothing in your time of need. . . Here we go.

Ahem. 'If I speak in the tongues of men or angels. . .'

Lilly Grant

The Irritating Gentleman

She laid her head to rest against the wood of the carriage and let her gaze unfocus itself against the passing countryside. She longed for the sun to turn itself red and for dusk to settle in; the night following shortly after and, with any grace, some solace after that.

All at once, she felt the shift behind her and saw smoke billow past her face.

'What, may I ask, is a young lass like yourself doing travelling all alone at this time of day?' husked the man in the space behind her ear.

She closed her eyes, asking the universe for an interruption, an unexpected turn of events. On he stumbled though, reeling off a lurid spew of whispers that was completely at odds with the beautiful countryside whishing past the window.

Her eyes slowly opened, and alongside the pang of regret that began to twist itself in her gut, the single tear that had been threatening to escape her since she reached the station that morning finally began to work its way out of its reddening corner.

'I know a grip-full of men who would–' (the man drew in a long toke of his cigar) 'be *more* than willing to... plunder such a fine treasu–'

The man's billow of smoke was cut short as Sophie snapped her head upwards and sank her teeth into his ruddy neck.

As ribbons of crimson erupted and sprayed the oak walls, the man did his best to scream, but to no avail. Within seconds, his lifeless body slumped over the seat partition and Sophie rose to her feet. Wiping the red from her face, she walked into the aisle and towards the door at the end of the carriage, pausing to meet the gaze of the sole passenger left on the train. The man's bewildered expression was almost comical: wide-eyed, mouth agape. An ember inside her longed to grin at this, to laugh at the horror of it all; but the overwhelming perfume of the moment, the flowers of guilt and shame that were blooming inside her, pulled her onwards without remark. She had taken a life again; had broken her oath *again*. She set her jaw, steeled her gaze, then opened the carriage door.

Sophie moved into the open air, and then with the grace of a prima donna, stepped off the moving platform.

Standing alone in the middle of the dusty rail track, she watched as her latest mistake, and the carnage with it, hurtled further into the distance.

Giften Etienne

The Irritating Gentleman

Dear Secretary of the Berlin Museum of Art,

I am writing to address concern over a painting by the gentleman Berthold Woltz that was recently unveiled in your gallery. I take great issue with the content of it, which I believe to be a depiction of myself at my most vulnerable moment. At the time, I was returning home from my beloved sister's funeral in Munich; I was travelling alone and could hardly contain my devastation. You can imagine my disgust when, as tears rolled down my eyes, a most repulsive man emerged from the seat behind me. I tried my best to ignore him as he made inappropriate advances toward me. It was deeply distressing.

Though I paid him no attention, I noticed that a bystander was scribbling something in his notebook as I was being harassed. I now believe the bystander in question was Sir Woltz scribbling down a sketch of my misery and that this sketch was the very first draft of his painting. Given this, I request that this painting, an immortalised portrait of the worst day of my life thus far, be removed from public viewing in the galleries.

Sincerely, Miss Ava Hoffman.

Theo Vaughan

Black is not a colour

Acquainted with the taste of coal mined from the depths of '*inferno*', the train rushed past the countryside, blurring the green works of Mother Nature into a second-long realist masterpiece. Its painters were those whose wealthy eyes dedicated themselves to the riches of beauty, whose calloused fingers had perhaps never picked up a brush before and whose colour was determined by the silence of their tears.

Black was, however, not a colour. Perhaps it was a shade of grief, of mourning tongues and anguished minds, a shade which bled from unspoken wounds and torn futures one could not return to. Black was a shawl, a dress darker than Death's cover. Black was, perhaps, Mother Nature's final lover.

What gentle babe this train rocks.

Black was not a colour. It was a shade of distress, of a troubled mind and anxious eyes, a shade that tears from grinning lips and unsanctioned palms. Black was a hideous veil, a dress that hid what Life has to offer. Black was, certainly, lust's coffer.

What gentle babe this man rocks.

Sofia Camara-Martins

The Irritating Gentleman

there is no governess,
no mother no father no family not clinging
just me and this acrid, sticking feeling
crawling up my spine and neck
like mucus in lungs.

there is no protector,
no person to trust or hold my hand,
not even the gentleman
who'd been conversing with
the looming figure over me now.

hot smoke and hotter breath curls 'bout my ears
caught in a nightmare i cannot wake from.
no blackened armour can shield me,
no steed nor knight will rescue me.

i wish for peace and comfort and silence and miss grey.

and still
the dragon billows his smoke,
hot sticking words like tar on my neck,
my throat is thick with phlegm and tears.
i bite my tongue.

my mind wanders to miss grey,
her warnings and advice and warmth.

'my dear, be gentle, but do not be weak.'

my fingers twitch.
i reach for my hat pin.

                                        Sinnead Singson

The Irritating Gentleman

The train rattled slightly on the railway tracks as the sound of groaning wood splintered my ears. I stared out at the window, observing the endless expanse of flashing trees with pained eyes. The corners of my eyes stung and I felt as though I were crushed under the weight of the umber dress and cloak left for me by my late mother. If only I could join her now, rather than spend the rest of my miserable existence en-route to her horrid brother's home. Alone.

My thoughts were permeated with another creak, this time beside my ear. The musky smell of cologne invaded my senses as I instinctively leaned closer to the window, clutching my handkerchief. The only remnant of her and a dreadful reminder of my wretched newfound reality.

'Greetings, little dove.'

I heard the smirk in his tone. Imagined too vividly the lurid gaze behind his spectacles.

'My friend and I wanted to extend an invitation to join us.' The man was now leaning his elbows on the back of my seat, leaning closer with that nauseating grin. He held a cigar between his fingers. 'Lots of unsavoury characters, who would prey on a pretty doll like you, darling. You would be much safer with gentlemen like us.'

My eyes wandered to you, stranger, with a breathless sigh, dreading the chasm of space between us – although you were a mere few steps away across the carriage. A silent tear slid down my cheek.

Sofija Vipule

The Irritating Gentleman

The fair-haired girl with plaits in front of me was skittish, like a fox caught in one of the night's yellowed streetlamps. Her head tweaked and turned from her window seat down to the furthest aisles of the train. My thumb traced the frayed butt-end of the last cigar in my pocket. The girl's behaviour seemed overtly irregular and, as time went on, the guilt was so thick in my throat I found myself lighting my final and only ailment to anxiety. I needed to prepare myself for instigating a polite conversation. My legs folded like tinned sardines as I rotated in my seat to kneel over the bench-head. I pulled my lips apart and threw up three words:

'Excuse me, miss?'

There was no distance between the moment I started speaking and the girl's neck rapidly contorting to face me. She had bee-sting eyelids and wet lips where tears had fallen and absorbed. She was committed to a black outfit, which highlighted the paleness of her skin. Her expression of pure grief was only emphasised as I tried to paste on my kindest visage. Something in her eyes itched my brain as to whether we knew each other. After this relentless, uncomfortable look had been shared for several seconds, she spoke.

'*You* are to blame.'

These words warped a bumpy scar of a memory into a fresh, throbbing infection.

Sadie Brett

The Irritating Gentleman

The balmy spring sun dappled the long oak table.

I was staring at the damask-patterned wallpaper. Otto sat on one of the brocade dining chairs, face down in the spargelsuppe. Franz and Helen were on the floor holding hands. Their eyes were still open. With a puppy-like tilt, I examined their mouths. It appeared as a phantasmagoria. As if they had swallowed dandelions. Tiny white feathers were floating in the air. Some were stuck on their chins. Caroline realised what I had done. 'Mörder,' she said. Killer. Her mouth was turning into an enormous cloud. A half choke, half vomit.

I pondered upon this recollection when I rubbed my eyes for the fourth time. Coetaneously, an audible disturbance reached my ears, originating in the carriage behind me. I turn to my right, look up and identify the subject of such impertinence. Pray, I find myself the object of pointed observations, a gentleman's gaze. How distressing! Yet, in the next moment, his gaze fixated upon my hand.

'Oh? Might I ask you to partake in a pfeffernusse cookie?'

A grin plays upon his features when he answers: 'Danke.'

I offer a smile and watch him take a bite. Watch the spectacle. Watch, lick his fingers one by one. Watch the cloud-like sugar on his moustache.

Adelina Cazacutu

The Irritating Gentleman

The sun beams through the window of the carriage, interrupted
only by the forest we are passing through.
I cannot stand it.
I cannot stop my silent weeping, nor I am sure I want to. I am
allowed to grieve, am I?
I hear a buzzing in my ear. Someone talking incessantly, a
gentleman. He is behind me, so I cannot see him, but I can smell
the cigarette he is certainly smoking.
If I could, I would break it into pieces.
I am not listening. I am lost in my memories, longing for one more
embrace from my mother. It will never happen again.
But this man...he is here, he talks to me and he is really pleased
with himself.
I wish harassing ladies and young girls on a train carriage was not
such a common thing. I long for the day it will happen.
If I don't answer, maybe he will stop.
I turn my head from the carriage window and I see him. A man
looking at me and stopping only to sketch on a notebook.
What is he seeing?

Amanda Mangolini

His White-Winged Angel

And there I sat,
His white-winged angel
His golden-headed girl
With eyes bluer than the seven seas
And lips as tempting as a secret summer kiss.

A year ago I might have smiled,
Might have blushed, might have giggled
Might have thanked the gentleman
For his spoken generosity

Back when I was simply a child,
A girl and not yet a woman.

A little girl would not see
That his words were not generous
Nor were they kind.
They were lustful, enunciated with desire;
Yes, his words were consumed by greed.

I am told I am a woman now
For little girls do not bleed
I am told that I must remain virtuous,
Untouched.

I do not understand why,

For he did not care for my black attire when he undressed me
Nor the tears I wept for my dear mama.
He simply desired his white-winged angel,
Yes, he wanted to degrade his golden-headed girl.

Zara Auckbaraullee

The Irritating Gentleman

Ello love, he prods the top of her seat.

Mind if I sit down?

. . .

Well, it doesn't matter really.

He takes a puff on his thin cigar, the smoke landing in her wispy, golden hair.

Sorry ta botha ya, darlin' but I'm with His Majesty's royal service ya see. Me and Old Leroy here. Isn't that right mate?

Umnnnh, his companion grunts.

See, we're going round to every lass in the land to see if their feet fits this crystal slipper here. You probably 'erd about it?–

He takes another suck on his cigar and coughs until he sees angels. Her continued silence seems like a violent stroke of entitlement to him.

The slipper, Leroy!

From his associate's musty pocket comes a dainty crystal wonder, blue in acidic technicolour, only slightly tarnished from nicotine-stained finger marks and splashes from hot soup.

Boy, are you all on your own? What's a pretty little doll like you all alone?

. . .

AHEM, he coughs. Not because he has to, rather to fill the silence.

Well, Madam, if you just remove your left shoe as so. . .

And Leroy's there kneeling at her feet as if about to kiss her flaky leather boots.

Madam?

. . .

Show me your feet, love, don't be shy!

The gentleman rubs his hands together after flicking his extinguished cigar butt out of the window. Inching towards her, he places himself onto the seat directly opposite her.

Now, let me see, quite a boot you have here. Lifting her entire, almost lifeless foot into his hand.

Let's get that off, shall we?

A tear seems to have found its way down her cheek, that much is clear about her. For the two gentlemen to mention it would only be an inconvenience.

Ooh, there we go – popping the boot off.

He strokes her sock before carefully peeling it away, the way a bride would reveal her face through the veil. Then gazing into her frail yellow foot, his nostrils expanding. Reeks like heaven, he thinks. Silently, Leroy bequeaths the slipper. How smooth it slides across the curve of her heel, but still the gentleman holds his breath as the crystal comes to encase it.

Well, I never. . . It fits. . . Well, Madam I'm. . .

But she rises from the wooden slab and that very movement is enough to make all his words remain thoughts, only opening his mouth to allow a thick whiskey scented gasp to escape. The very humid air of the train rumbles and, from the view of her upturned face from below, it seems that she could destroy anything.

All the singeing of a seal being pressed into hot wax, the foot bearing the crystal slipper stamping directly into the gentleman's face, the face that's trying to smooch the heel. And to all the many passengers seated nearby, it was unclear if his mangled gargles were of pleasure or of pain.

Harper Stringer

CREATIVE WRITING PROMPT 4

Writing Dialogue: an Argument

Using Shakespeare's *Richard III* as a reference point, rewrite the dialogue set in the present as an argument between the Princes William and Harry.

Alternatively, think of an argument that you've had. Write it as a dialogue or as a script for a play.

If you are writing a dialogue, consider how you will present the turn-taking, i.e. as direct speech, free direct speech, as a screenplay, etc. What about *powerful v powerless* features, politeness strategies and other features of dialogue discussed in class.

An argument

A sighs.

B: What now?

A: What's that supposed to mean?

B: What do you mean/

A: /I just don't know why you said it like that.

B: How else was I meant to say it?
Look, y– you might just be hungry let's...

A: I ate.

B: Okay.

B: I'm uh...seeing my dad on Friday.

A nods, there is thick air between them.

B: Is this the part where you ask me to leave again? Where I make
it halfway out the door before you call me to come back?

A: No. I'm not upset, don't act like I am.

B sighs.

A: What are you doing on Friday?

B: told you I'm seeing my dad/

A: /I know, I mean what are you doing with him/

B: /Were you even listening?

A: I was! I'm asking what you're doing with him.
B: Okay, I'm sorry.
A: What are you apologising for? We're just having a discussion/
B: /I don't know, it seems I always have something to apologise for
so I'll just get it out of the way I guess.

A rolls her eyes. They are stood in the kitchen, at least 3 feet between them. B breaks the distance. They lock eyes and he realises this is a bad idea.

B: I'm going for a drive/
A: /I'm going to bed.

They walk separate ways, she puts the kettle on and he grabs his keys.

B: I'll be back in maybe 30 minutes.
A: Okay, I might be asleep by then – lock up when you get back.

B nods, throws a coat on as she turns to face him, leaning on the counter.

B: I love you.
A: Mm, I love you too.

Danica Ignacio

Keeping Score

I looked into his gleaming eyes and tried in vain to bite back the smile tickling my cheeks.

'You're just lucky.'

'No. You're just in denial about the fact that I'm better. We've played this game fifty-nine times now.'

'Yeah and I've won thirty times.'

'Sure. But in the last thirty games we've played, you've lost 95 per cent of them.'

'So?' He shuffled the cards as I glared at him. 'I'm still in the lead.'

'Sure, but the first, like, 23 points were just a handicap.'

I scoffed, turning away from the proud gleam in his eyes. 'No way.'

'But good job for holding up so well against me when I'm using only 2 per cent of my brain power,' his lips smirked in amusement as he continued to shuffle the cards. 'Not everyone can do that.'

I smiled, still looking away as I folded my arms over my chest. 'You're so silly.'

'Do you want to keep playing?' He then checked the time on his laptop screen and laughed.

'I remember you saying about an hour ago that we would play until you won two games.'

He then turned back to raise an eyebrow at me. 'I've just been destroying you the entire time.'

I scoffed, nodding at the cards in his hands as I stretched. 'I can win this. Let's play.'

I didn't. The score ended up being 31–32. Still counting.

Sofija Vipule

Harry Dies On An Impossible Hill

The King, dressed in his robes and crown,
lounges around his drawing room alone,
a goblet of brandy in his hand, when his son, Harry, enters.

Harry: Father, I must ask you something.
King: Ask, ask, ask. Your wish is not mine to grant.
Harry: It's regarding Uncle Andrew, father.

The King begins picking at his fingernails

Harry: I'm quite sorry to bring it up.
King: I sense a *but*, my son. . .
Harry: Well, don't you think we ought to say something?
King: Ah, there lies the problem. It is not a question of *we* anymore, is it?
Harry: My name will always be Windsor, will it not?
King: I cannot read the tea leaves, but I believe, boy, that I know right from wrong. My brother's business is not our own.
Harry: Well, Golly!
King: It seems to me that your generation is dead set on turning shadows into ghosts, seeing dangers where they don't exist Great men have been renamed with the titles of famous sinners. It's only a matter of time before everyone is caught with their trousers down.

The King crosses himself and strokes the fur of his crown

Harry: But what about right and wrong?

King: There's no morality where the light doesn't shine.

Harry: Father! I fear the crown has done dreadful things to you. But then again, perhaps you have good reason to be afraid.

King: Now, stop that.

Harry: What did you get up to, Pa? All those days away from me and mother dearest.

King: Nonsense, balderdash. Haemorrhoids. Little dog's turds. It must be all those ghastly pills, powders and flowers that make you say these things.

Harry: What tosh! And how foolish you seem in your ill-fitting garbs, as if you're a little boy trying on your parent's clothes. Well, then again. I suppose you are. . .

King: Calm yourself, boy, maintain your decency! (*To Servant*) JAMESON! FETCH THE DOCTOR. Be still, devil-boy!

The King begins following his son into a corner of the room.

Harry: No, this is not the end. I know things, father.

King: I'm sure you know many things. Nouns, cars, disciples, preservatives. You're just not strong enough to comprehend them.

Harry: My book will hear about it!

King: Tut, tut, tut.

Harry: The whole world will know what you've done!

King: (*To Doctor*) Ah, Doctor. Nice to see you. We've got a little stint of hysteria here.

Doctor: I can see that. He's gone all yellow.

King: Yes, I thought that.

Harry: I'm not yellow, you're both green!

The King places his forefinger on Harry's lips

King: Hush hush, now.

Doctor: Yes, do what your good father says.

King: Now, Doctor. Zap him!

Harper Stringer

CREATIVE WRITING PROMPT 5

Your Fairy Tale

Take a well-known fairy tale and rewrite it by thinking about the prompts discussed in today's workshop on the Short Story and the Fairy Tale, e.g. by starting in the middle, with a flashback, choosing a different narrator / point of view, updating the setting, undermining schematic expectations, etc. Make your version as original and as unconventional as you like but readers should still be able to recognise the plot and characters. Your fairy tale can be up to *800 words*.

Big Bad Bloody Wolf

I ate the nice old lady who lived in this house.

I didn't mean to. I couldn't help it. Whenever the full moon comes out, I pass out and I usually wake up in a field with some pigs' bodies. Not now.

I'm still holding what's left – her bones; most of them still have flesh on them, have been ripped off her torso with the guts leaking out, the ones I haven't eaten yet. I left the head untouched, for some reason. It's still attached.

Her eyes looked so very kind before. They were light brown but, in the light, I could see they were ever so slightly green around the edges. They gleamed too. They're not reflecting any light anymore. They're grey now. There's nothing there. Oh God, she's not there.

She let me in yesterday evening, nursed me back to health, made me soup, let me sleep the night. This poor sweet woman didn't know she'd let in a beast that would butcher her. She made jokes with me – trusted me. She told me about her gardening and how she sold the flowers she grew. She told me that her granddaughter started taking the flowers into town because she couldn't walk safely anymore. She told–

Oh God.

That girl is going to come home to find a man covered in her grandmother's blood standing over her maimed corpse. What will I do then? I can't even imagine looking her in the eye. I think – I think I'll hide. . .

Theo Vaughan

The Evil Queen

'Sing, Goddess, of the Queen's coldness,
Miserly; tight fisted, that cost her husband
Incalculable pain. The Queen who
Starved and froze herself to death
And left her body to rot as a feast
For dogs and birds, and the King to remarry.'

Begin with the clash between Snow White and her stepmother, referred to as The Evil Queen. Snow White would insist on the basement as her dwellings after the lessons of the dead Queen who never lit the furnace and kept all the family finery in a cupboard under the stairs. The new Queen was not a harlot but sought beauty as an armour; they all saw her as vain but her scarlet crepe de chine gowns were her only solace. It appeared to The Queen that Snow White's modesty was an artifice as much as any trick a con artist would pull. The Queen sought to destroy the barrier between interior and exterior. Her only sins were not hidden away shamefully and the shallow mask of manners had been dropped.

Not even The Queen's mirror was capable of recognising her beauty. The magic mirror proclaimed Snow White the fairest and people far and wide bought into her show of cheap modesty. For this reason, one clear winter morning, Snow White rose from her basement to venture into the nearby villages to be amongst like-minded folk, not just any folk but her adoring fans. Leaving no note or mention of her plan, The Queen sent a friend into the wilds to look for her. On being found, she pulled a stunt where she fainted or at least pretended to. Finding this out, The Queen decided that it was perhaps time for Snow White to make her own mistakes. The magic mirror ceased to taunt her with her stepdaughter's beauty and a slight chill of calm came upon the kingdom.

If necessary to categorise time, ten years passed. Snow White had imposed herself onto the company of seven dwarves who had become so intoxicated with love that they would do anything for her. Meanwhile, the Queen's long silent magic mirror began taunting her with Snow White's *good nature*. It appeared that her stepdaughter still lived, and deciding to let old dogs lie, the Queen ventured into the villages to visit her. How sombre the villagers seemed yawning, dropping to their knees with the little enthusiasm they harboured. Venturing further into the bushy thickery, The Queen saw fists shaking in her face, and the unpleasant releases of sneers and whispers from beneath the shelter of shady trees out of sight to her. The further she travelled, the more common the sneers became; she reached a small mining town where even the grass was trampled with soot and phlegm and saw many sad faces ashy from blasted coal and rubble.

A crowd of coughing and scornful tears centred itself somewhere in the distance. The Queen didn't doubt for a second that Snow White had something to do with it. Hiding in a corner as close as she could get, The Queen caught sight of a kind of glass coffin and in it her stepdaughter, apparently dead.

'It's so sweet! Her body isn't decomposing or anything,' a villager proclaimed.

But The Queen could see that since the glass was all fogged up, Snow White was clearly breathing and was making trouble with some cruel trick or another.

'Everyone! The Evil Queen has been spotted nearby!' A young boy yelled, jumping upon a tree stump. In response came countless cries of shock.

'She comes back to gloat after killing her daughter!'

At which point, The Queen understood that for her own safety, it was best to make a quick exit. The most difficult thing on the planet was convincing someone that they had been lied to. But on turning, she saw that she was in the midst of a silent swarm of Snow White's angry minions, who had been waiting wordlessly for the right moment to strike.

So down came the net. The Queen was placed in an iron cage at the centre of the town. *'How dya like being an object of vanity, now?'* They all asked her. She was stripped of her gowns and makeup, reduced to plain rags. A silhouette of her once painted face melted to the floor which she slept on, the last remnants of a beautiful past.

A few days later, a visiting Prince happened upon Snow White, gave her a peck on the lips, and her life was restored. The romance of stirring cherry blossoms falling from the branches was only a foreshadowing of the violence to come. Snow White came upon the iron cage to face her stepmother.

'This decay was only inevitable,' she tutted.

'Perhaps that is true. But my spirit is intact whereas yours withered long ago. Your modesty has taken you nowhere but the total deterioration of your humanity.'

Not knowing how to answer, Snow White forced The Queen into a magic mirror and had it blessed by a witch so that she was unable to escape. Unable to even die, The Queen spoke her every empty word in verse. Growing bitter, she taunted her stepdaughter just as her own mirror had done to her. The dust settled and she was unable to decline further, but Snow White grew old and repulsive with The Prince, going about her saintly aspirations and proclaiming ugliness as her religion.

(Note – The intro is appropriated from the opening lines of Homer's *Iliad*.)

Harper Stringer

Biography

Marina Lambrou is an Associate Professor in English Language and Linguistics and the Course Leader for BA Creative Writing and BA Creative Writing and Film Cultures at Kingston University.

She has over 30 publications in the areas of stylistics (literary language), narratology (including personal and trauma experiences), disnarration and teaching pedagogy. Her books include '*Narrative Retellings: Stylistic Approaches*', '*Disnarration and the Unmentioned in Fact and Fiction*' and '*Contemporary Stylistics*'. She is the Editor-in-Chief of the *Journal of Literary Semantics* (De Gruyter) and was a previous Chair of the *Poetics and Linguistics Association*, an international Association for research and study in literary language.

In 2023, she was appointed as a Quality Assurance Agency for Higher Education (QAA) Advisory Group member for Creative Writing to review and produce the new Subject Benchmark Statement.

About KUP

Kingston University Press has been publishing high-quality commercial and academic titles for over ten years. Our list has always reflected the diverse nature of the student and academic bodies at the university in ways that are designed to impact on debate, to hear new voices, to generate mutual understanding and to complement the values to which the university is committed.

Increasingly the books we publish are produced by students on the MA Publishing and BA Publishing courses, often working with partner organisations to bring projects to life. While keeping true to our original mission, and maintaining our wide-ranging backlist titles, our most recent publishing focuses on bringing to the fore voices that reflect and appeal to our community at the university as well as the wider reading community of readers and writers in the UK and beyond.

@KU_press

This book was edited, designed, typeset and produced by a student on the MA Publishing course at Kingston University, London.

To find out more about our hands-on, professionally focused and flexible MA and BA programmes please visit:

www.kingston.ac.uk

www.kingstonpublishing.wordpress.com

@kingstonjourno

www.ingramcontent.com/pod-product-compliance
Lightning Source LLC
Chambersburg PA
CBHW071234170626
46809CB00008BA/3056